W9-BCD-665

FELICITY
TAKES A DARE

FELICITY · 1774

BY VALERIE TRIPP

ILLUSTRATIONS DAN ANDREASEN

VIGNETTES SUSAN MCALILEY

THE AMERICAN GIRLS COLLECTION®

Published by Pleasant Company Publications
Previously published in *American Girl*® magazine
© Copyright 2001 by Pleasant Company

All rights reserved. No part of this book may be used or reproduced in
any manner whatsoever without written permission except in the case of
brief quotations embodied in critical articles and reviews.

For information, address: Book Editor, Pleasant Company Publications,
8400 Fairway Place, P.O. Box 620998, Middleton, WI 53562.

Printed in Singapore.
01 02 03 04 05 06 07 08 TWP 10 9 8 7 6 5 4 3 2 1

The American Girls Collection® and logo, American Girls Short Stories,™
the American Girl logo, Felicity,® and Felicity Merriman®
are trademarks of Pleasant Company.

Edited by Nancy Holyoke and Michelle Jones
Designed by Joshua Mjaanes and Laura Moberly
Art Directed by Kym Abrams, Julie Mierkiewicz, and Joshua Mjaanes

Library of Congress Cataloging-in-Publication Data

Tripp, Valerie, 1951-
Felicity takes a dare / by Valerie Tripp ;
illustrations, Dan Andreasen ; vignettes, Susan McAliley.
p. cm. — (The American girls collection)
Summary: All winter Felicity has waited to go to the
Williamsburg town fair, but her foolhardy actions in trying
to feed the racehorses spoil the fun and teach her a lesson.

ISBN 1-58485-271-2
[1. Behavior—Fiction. 2. Fairs—Fiction. 3. Williamsburg (Va.)—
History—Colonial period, ca. 1600–1774—Fiction.]
I. Andreasen, Dan, ill. II. McAliley, Susan, ill. III. Title. IV. Series.
PZ7.T7363 Feke 2001   [Fic]—dc21   00-032651

The
AMERICAN GIRLS
COLLECTION ®

OTHER AMERICAN GIRLS
SHORT STORIES:

JOSEFINA'S SONG

KIRSTEN SNOWBOUND!

ADDY'S WEDDING QUILT

SAMANTHA AND THE
MISSING PEARLS

MOLLY MARCHES ON

PICTURE CREDITS

The following individuals and organizations have generously given
permission to reprint illustrations contained in "Looking Back":
p. 32—Illustration by Susan Moore; pp. 34–35—Colonial Williamsburg Foundation;
p. 36—© Bettmann/CORBIS; pp. 37–38—Colonial Williamsburg Foundation;
p. 40—Photography by Jamie Young and prop styling by Jean doPico;
pp. 46–47—Illustration by D. J. Simison.

TABLE OF CONTENTS

FATHER
*Felicity's father, who owns
one of the general stores
in Williamsburg.*

MOTHER
*Felicity's mother, who
takes care of her family
with love and pride.*

FELICITY
*A spunky, spritely
colonial girl, growing
up just before the
American Revolution.*

NAN

Felicity's sweet and sensible sister, who is six years old.

WILLIAM

Felicity's almost-three brother, who likes mischief and mud puddles.

FELICITY
TAKES A DARE

Look at me!" cried Felicity Merriman. "I'm a high-wire dancer, just like at the fair!" Felicity climbed onto the fence as her sister Nan and brother William watched. The old fence was unsteady, but Felicity held her arms out from her sides, found her balance, and walked heel-toe, heel-toe along the top of it. Then she stood on one foot and gracefully pointed the toe of the other foot in front of her.

"You do look like the high-wire dancers, Lissie," said Nan. "Oh, I can't wait to see them at the fair today!"

"I want to see everything," said Felicity. "Especially the racehorses."

All through the winter, everyone in Williamsburg looked forward to the spring fair. People came to town from far and near to enjoy the music and dancing, to see the prize animals, and to watch the races and contests. Today the fair was finally here, and no one was more excited than Felicity. She rose up on her toes now and spun around to walk along the shaky fence in the other direction.

"Hurrah!" shouted Nan and William. They clapped and cheered so loudly,

"You do look like the high-wire dancers, Lissie," said Nan.

Mrs. Merriman came rushing from the house to see what all the commotion was about. When she saw Felicity teetering atop the rickety fence, Mrs. Merriman gasped.

"Felicity!" she said. "Come down at once! What dangerous nonsense!"

Felicity jumped to the ground and landed with a thud. "I'm sorry, Mother," she said.

"I should think so!" Mrs. Merriman said. "You should have more sense. What if you had fallen?"

"Oh," Felicity began, trying to reassure her mother. "I'm never afraid of falling—"

"But you *should* be!" interrupted Mrs. Merriman. "And what sort of an example are you setting for Nan and William? If I had not come out when I did, you would have been helping them to walk the fence, too, I've no doubt." She shook her head. "You must learn the difference between being brave and being foolhardy, or someday you will do yourself or someone else real harm."

"Yes, Mother," said Felicity. To herself she said, *I wouldn't have fallen! Walking on the fence isn't dangerous for me. And I never would have let Nan or William try it. I know that there are lots of things I can do that they cannot do. Why, just today Father said that I could go with him to the fireworks at the fair tonight. Nan and William are much too young to do that.*

Mrs. Merriman looked at Felicity and sighed. "Run along inside now," she said. "You, too, Nan and William. Tidy yourselves. Then we'll walk to the fair." She smiled a little smile that had both love and exasperation in it. "But we'll walk on the ground and *not* on the fences, if you please!"

✿

The streets were crowded with people heading toward Market Square, the big, open space in the middle of Williamsburg where tents and booths were set up. Felicity smelled wood smoke and heard laughter

and music well before she could see
the fair. She skipped ahead of Mother,
pulling Nan along.

"Felicity," Mrs. Merriman warned.
"Stay close to me."

"Look, Mother!" exclaimed Felicity
when she saw a crowd gathering by the
running field. "A footrace is starting. May
we watch?"

Mother lifted William so he could
see the racers line up. Felicity and Nan
both shrieked with surprise at the
loud *bang!* of the starting gun.
They jumped and cheered
so much that when the
race was over, they felt
as if they'd run it, too.

Felicity wanted to go look for the horses, but just then a group of tumblers appeared on the field. Nan clapped with delight and William tried to imitate their somersaults. After the tumblers, the high-wire dancers began. The children watched wide-eyed as the dancers balanced on a wire strung between two poles.

"Gracious!" exclaimed Mother. "Just looking at the high wire makes me dizzy. Come along to the fiddlers' tent. Let's

listen to the music."

Mother, Felicity, and Nan clapped their hands and tapped their feet to the fiddle music, but William covered his ears. "Too squeaky!" he said.

*The children watched wide-eyed as the dancers balanced
on a wire strung between two poles.*

Felicity was happy when they finally came to the pens for the prizewinning farm animals. She knew the racehorses must be nearby. She and Nan and William mooed at the cows and gasped at the size of the huge oxen. The children admired the prize pig, who was fat and pink and peaceful, and laughed aloud at the way the prize chickens fluttered and fussed.

At a gaily decorated booth, Mother bought the children treats. Nan chose a tart. William chose gingerbread, which he immediately dropped. Felicity was too excited about seeing the horses to be hungry. She gave William some of the little cakes she had chosen and put the rest in her pocket.

Mother was dusting crumbs off William when her friend Mrs. Fitchett greeted her.

"Good day, Mrs. Fitchett," said Mrs. Merriman with a smile.

Mrs. Fitchett beamed. "Well, children, I'm sure you are enjoying the fair," she said. "And Mrs. Merriman, have you seen the display of embroidery stitches, new from London? Come, I'll show you."

Felicity's heart sank. *Oh no!* she thought. *Not stitches! Not now, just when we're finally going to see the horses!*

"Please, Mother," she blurted out. "May Nan and William and I go look at the horses? They're just over there." Felicity pointed to a grassy pasture surrounded by a wooden fence.

Mrs. Merriman started to say, "No, I—"

"Oh, let them go," cut in Mrs. Fitchett. "They'll come to no harm."

Mrs. Merriman hesitated. Then she said to the children, "Very well. I'll fetch you in a little while. Stay together."

"We will!" Felicity assured her. She hurried Nan and William over to the horse pen as fast as their legs could go.

Nan sat down on a stump to finish eating her tart, and William found a stick to poke into a mud puddle. Felicity leaned against the fence and shaded her eyes. She loved to look at horses. And these were not rough farm horses but sleek racehorses with slender legs and glossy coats. They trotted rest-lessly around the pen,  tossing their shiny manes and flicking their long tails.

Felicity often rode the horses on her grandfather's plantation when she visited there. She was proud of the way she could make friends with horses. Grandfather had taught her to treat

13

horses with respect, and they trusted her. She knew how to be loving and calm, especially with high-strung horses like these, which were easily upset by loud noises or sudden movement.

For a while, Felicity studied the horses in the pen, trying to decide which one she'd choose for her own if she could. She was jolted out of her daydream by a pack of noisy boys coming up to the pen. She recognized some of them from church, though they were certainly acting differently here. They ripped up handfuls of grass, waved them, and shouted at the horses to come eat from their hands. The nervous horses trotted away to the farthest corner of the pen, but the boys ran after them outside the fence, still yelling.

Nan and William stood up and moved closer to Felicity. She glared at the boys and frowned fiercely. "You boys!" she said. "Stop!"

A few of the boys quieted down, but the largest one smirked at Felicity. "What's the matter, little girl?" he asked. "Are the horses scaring you?"

"No!" said Felicity. "I am not the least bit scared of the horses."

"You are, too," said the boy.

"I am not," said Felicity, furious.

"Well, then," said the boy. "If you're so brave, I dare you to feed one of them."

Felicity hesitated. A small voice inside her warned that it was foolish to

"Well, then," said the boy. "If you're so brave,
I dare you to feed one of them."

take any dare, and that taking this one would be downright dangerous, because she did not know these horses. Felicity shook her head. *But making friends with horses is not risky for me,* she said to herself. *It's something I'm very good at.*

"Go on," said the boy. "I dare you."

Without another thought, Felicity jumped over the fence and into the pen. The horses eyed her, tossing their heads and shifting anxiously.

"Go on," said the boy.

"Be quiet," Felicity hissed. Slowly, she took the little cakes out of her pocket and stretched her arm out toward the horses, the cakes in her open palm. Muscles twitched in the horses' legs and necks as they watched her.

Felicity walked steadily forward. "Look what I have for you," she murmured. The horses pricked their ears toward her. "Don't be afraid," she said softly. "See? Cakes."

Slowly, Felicity walked closer and closer to the horses. She could smell them. She could feel the earth tremble when they stamped their feet and backed away from her. Still she walked closer.

One horse stretched out its neck toward her. Felicity stood absolutely still. The horse took one step and then another nearer to her. Felicity held her hand steady. Slowly, the horse bent its head lower. She could feel its warm breath on her hand.

When the horse leaned down and began to eat the cakes out of her hand, Felicity turned her head to flash a triumphant look at the boys.

BOOM! A gunshot cracked the air. Felicity thought, *They must be starting another race.* Then everything happened at once. The horse eating out of her hand reared up and kicked its front feet wildly. Felicity shrank back. At the same time the other horses charged toward her, madly scrambling, running into one another, snorting, lunging every which way.

"Lissie!" screamed Nan. Felicity turned to run, but one of the horses brushed past her so that she stumbled, then another knocked her down to the

The horse reared up and kicked its front feet wildly.
Felicity shrank back.

wet, cold ground with such force that she lay gasping. She tried to pick herself up, but another horse thundering past kicked her arm so hard Felicity heard a crack. A stab of pain shot up her arm. There was a rushing sound in her ears. Nan's cries and the boys' shouts seemed far away.

Felicity bit her lip to keep from crying out and struggled to her feet. By now the horses were on the far side of the pen. Felicity staggered toward the fence, bent over, holding her hurt arm to her chest. She didn't stop until she had crawled through the fence, out of the pen. Then she slumped against a fence pole, looked at Nan's frightened face, and whispered, "Go get Mother."

❦

Felicity was carried home and put to bed. Mr. Galt, the apothecary, was sent for. When he walked into the room, Mother said softly, "Lissie, my love, Mr. Galt is here to see to your arm now."

Felicity sat up, but the pain was so great she gasped.

"Lie back," said Mr. Galt kindly. "Move slowly, or it will hurt."

Mr. Galt told Mother to hold Felicity's elbow and wrist. He grasped Felicity's forearm where it was most swollen. Gently but firmly, he pulled with his hands. "I'm moving the bone back into place," he said. It hurt so much, Felicity couldn't help whimpering.

"You've a simple break," Mr. Galt explained. "But there's quite a bit of swelling. I'm going to use leeches to bring the swelling down."

Felicity closed her eyes. She couldn't bear to watch Mr. Galt put the dark leeches on her skin. She felt tiny bites on her arm as the leeches attached themselves and then began sucking the blood from her swollen bruises.

When the swelling had gone down, Mr. Galt removed the leeches. They were fat with blood. He put a splint on Felicity's arm and tied it securely with a wide bandage. Then he slipped Felicity's arm into a sling made of leather lined with wool. "Your mother may bathe your

23

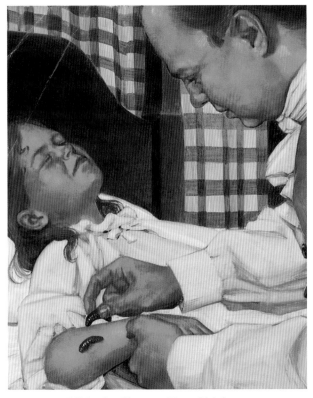

*Felicity closed her eyes. She couldn't bear to
watch Mr. Galt put the dark leeches on her skin.*

arm from time to time," he said. "But otherwise you must keep your arm in the sling day and night for six weeks and try not to move it at all."

Mr. Galt gave Felicity some medicine to help her sleep. As she closed her eyes, he said, "Don't worry, Mrs. Merriman. Felicity's arm should mend quickly and well."

When Felicity woke up a few hours later, Mother was sitting next to her bed. She asked quietly, "How do you feel, Lissie?"

Felicity swallowed hard. She knew Mother was asking how her arm felt, but she chose to answer, "I feel ashamed. Taking the dare was a foolish thing to do."

"Nan told me about the boy," said Mother. "He was wrong to dare you."

"I was wrong," said Felicity. Her eyes filled with tears. "I didn't think your warning was meant for me, but it was. You were right, Mother. I'm not brave, I'm just foolhardy."

"No, my love," said Mother. "I saw you be very brave when Mr. Galt was setting your arm."

"I was so looking forward to going to the fireworks with Father tonight," said Felicity. "I was so proud of finally being old enough to go."

"Come," said Mother. Carefully, she helped Felicity into a chair by the window. "You'll see the fireworks from here.

That will cheer you."

Mother was right. A brilliant burst of yellow light lit the dark sky, and the sight did make Felicity feel better. She brushed the tears off her cheeks and smiled. "Thank you, Mother," she said.

"That's my good girl," said Mother. Then she grinned. "And here is something to cheer *me*. I can be sure I won't see you walking on any fences for a while!"

Felicity and her mother laughed. Then they sat in the dark room together, watching fireworks streak across the night sky.

VALERIE TRIPP

At 9   Now

When I was eight, a carnival came to our town. Our family went the first night. I liked the Ferris wheel best. From the top, I could look down on the lights of our town twinkling in the summer night. It was as if there were stars above me and below me, too.

Valerie Tripp has written thirty-six books in The American Girls Collection, including nine about Felicity.

LOOKING
BACK
1774

A PEEK INTO
THE PAST

The fair in Felicity's story takes place
during Publick Times, when Virginia's high-
est court was in session in Williamsburg.
There were so many visitors during Publick
Times that Williamsburg's population
almost doubled overnight. Colonists came
to hear the trials in the
courts of law and to hear

*Colonists held Publick
Times just as they had
in England.*

the news of the town and the colonies.
They came to learn about the latest
clothing, music, amusements, and ideas
from Europe.

Visitors often gathered in shops like
Mr. Merriman's. They chatted with the
townspeople, local farmers, and wagon
drivers and boatmen who brought news
from the towns they had passed through.
Visitors also listened to crew members of
sailing ships talk of their adventures in

faraway places like Africa, South America, and the West Indies.

During Publick Times the taverns were so crowded they were often overflowing. Visitors went there to talk about business and to catch up on the news. Many of the men who visited Williamsburg stayed in

Taverns were filled with laughter, music, and the smell of good food.

the taverns. But there were so many people that they often had to share their beds. Visiting women did not stay in taverns. They usually stayed with relatives or friends.

While court was in session, the fair was held in Market Square, the center of Williamsburg. This was the town *common*, or the place where the townspeople gathered together. During the fair, the square was full of activity—there were many things to see and do! Booths and tents were set up all around the square. Some of them had animals, fruits, and vegetables that farmers from the outskirts of town brought into Williamsburg to sell. Servants from fine homes bartered with the farmers over the price of cabbages, chickens, and other livestock. Some booths had displays of embroidery and

merchandise just in from London, and others sold tarts, cakes, or gingerbread. Sometimes *peddlers*, people who sold things like pots and pans and tools on the street or door-to-door, came to Market Square, too. A girl like Felicity might find a peddler selling a toy that whirled in the wind, a kite with a colorful tail, or a wooden cup-and-ball game.

As people strolled around

34

Market Square, they might see exotic animals, jugglers, puppeteers, and acrobats performing. Fairgoers could listen to fiddlers playing lively music or stop and watch people dancing reels and jigs.

There were also all kinds of exciting games, contests, and races to see. The horse races began with the *bang!* of a starting gun, and the cheering crowd could be heard around the square. One popular contest was trying to catch a pig whose tail was lathered with slippery soap! People also watched beauty contests, footraces, and soldiers marching by.

Each night of Publick Times, there were plays and parties. The plays were sometimes funny and sometimes tragic.

Some of them were written by William Shakespeare, England's most famous playwright. Actors might travel all the way from London and bring their own scenery and fancy costumes. The ladies and

William Shakespeare

gentlemen of Virginia were treated to the same grand performances enjoyed by sophisticated London audiences. During Publick Times, George Washington and Thomas Jefferson were often seen attending popular plays.

*Mrs. Nancy Hallam, acting here in Shakespeare's play **Cymbeline,** was an actress admired by many, including George Washington.*

A ball at the Governor's Palace

The parties were some of the most elegant balls of the year. The fanciest was at the Governor's Palace. At a governor's ball, the guests were served a formal dinner in the late afternoon. The ladies dined first. Then the servants reset the table, the gentlemen took their seats, and the meal began again. While the men ate, the ladies chatted on the terrace or strolled through the gardens.

In the ballroom, the dancing began under the light of the glittering chandeliers, and a string quartet played the newest music from Europe. The music became livelier throughout the evening, until the drivers arrived to take the guests home. The next evening, many guests returned for a second night of dancing!

At the end of the fair, a colorful, glittering fireworks show lit up the night sky. Everyone gathered to "ooh" and "aahh" at the fair's glorious grand finale!

AN
AMERICAN
GIRLS
PASTIME

PLAY QUOITS

Have fun with a game of colonial horseshoes.

Felicity loved Publick Times and the excitement of Market Square. There were so many kinds of entertainment, such as tumblers, high-wire dancers, and race-horses. There were also footraces and games such as *quoits*. Quoits is similar to horseshoes and was popular during colonial times. It's also a game Felicity might have liked to play.

Make your own game of quoits, and invite your friends to play!

YOU WILL NEED:

2 wooden dowels

8 small embroidery hoops

2 colors of paint

Paintbrushes

*2 wooden **finials**,
or decorative tops (optional)*

Glue

Yardstick

To make the game:

1. The dowels are the *hobs,* or posts, and the embroidery hoops are the *quoits,* or rings.

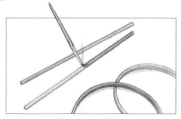

2. Paint one dowel and 4 hoops one color. Paint the other dowel and the 4 remaining hoops the other color. If you are using finials, paint them to match the dowels. Then glue them to the tops of the dowels.

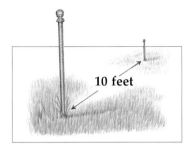

10 feet

3. Push one hob into the ground. Push the other hob into the ground 10 feet from the first hob.

To play the game:

1. The players divide into 2 teams. Each team chooses a color and stands by its hob.

2. Team A tosses quoits to Team B's hob.

3. Team B tosses quoits to Team A's hob.

4. Teams get a point for every quoit that rings the hob. The first team to get 10 points wins.

Turn the page to see how the game is played.